EOIN COLFER'S
Legend of . . .
SPUD MURPHY

EOIN COLFER'S
Legend of...
SPUD MURPHY

by EOIN COLFER
Illustrated by GLENN McCOY

miramax books

Hyperion Paperbacks for Children/New York

Text copyright © 2004 by Eoin Colfer
Illustrations copyright © 2004 by Glenn McCoy
All rights reserved. No part of this book may be reproduced or transmitted in any form or by any means, electronic or mechanical, including photocopying, recording, or by any information storage and retrieval system, without written permission from the publisher. For information address Hyperion Books for Children, 114 Fifth Avenue, New York, New York 10011-5690.
First U.S. Paperback Edition, 2005
3 5 7 9 10 8 6 4
Printed in the United States of America
ISBN 0-7868-5501-0 (trade)—ISBN 0-7868-4911-8 (special market)
Library of Congress Cataloging-in-Publication data on file.
Visit www.hyperionbooksforchildren.com

To Seán:
welcome to Number 1

Contents

The Legend of
SPUD MURPHY

CHAPTER 1

UGLY FRANK

I've got four brothers. Imagine that. Five boys under eleven all living in the same house.

On wet summer days, our house gets very crowded. If we each bring two friends home, then there could be fifteen of us crammed into the house. At least eight will be roaring like lunatics, and the rest will be dying to go to the toilet. The flusher on our toilet snaps off about once every three months.

When my dad came home one day and found three sons and four strangers covered with war paint, swinging on the bedroom curtains, he decided that something had to be done. It didn't help that the war paint was stolen from Mom's makeup box.

"No more bringing friends home!" Dad declared after the warriors' parents had collected them.

"That's not fair," said Marty, the biggest brother, mascara streaking his cheeks.

"That punishment really affects me because I'm popular, but Will's best friend is his Action Man."

Will. That's me. I love that Action Man.

Donnie, Bert, and HP started complaining, too. But only because they're little brothers, and that's what little brothers do for a living. I know that technically I'm a little brother, too, but I'm in the big-brother half of the family.

Having one little brother is bad enough,

but having three is too much punishment for one person. That's enough punishment for an entire housing development. The trouble with little brothers is that they are never blamed for anything. All Donnie, Bert, and HP have to do is bat their blue eyes and let their bottom lips wobble a bit, and they are forgiven for everything. Donnie, Bert, and HP could stick an ax in my head and they'd still get off with ten minutes' no TV and a stern look. The only things that Marty and I ever agree on is that our three younger brothers are spoiled rotten.

"This house is a madhouse," said Dad.

"And he's the chief lunatic," I said, pointing to Marty.

"I'm not the one talking to dolls," retorted Marty.

That hurt. "Action Man is not a doll."

"Quiet!" said Dad through gritted teeth. "There must be something we can find for

you to do during the summer. Something to get you out of the house."

"Not my babies," said Mom, hugging the younger-brother squad tightly. They gave her the full baby treatment—big baby eyes, gap-tooth smiles—and HP even sucked his thumb. That kid has no shame.

"Maybe not those three. But Will and Marty are nine and ten now. We can find something for them. Something educational."

Marty and I groaned. Educational hobbies are the worst kind. They're like school during the summer.

Marty tried to save us. "Remember the last educational hobby? The art classes. I was sick for days."

"That was your own fault," said Mom.

"I only had a drink of water."

"You are not supposed to drink the water that people use to wash their brushes."

Dad was thinking. "What about the library?" he said, finally.

"What about it?" I said, trying to sound casual, but my stomach was churning.

"You both could join. Reading. It's perfect. How can you cause trouble reading a book?"

"Yes, of course, it's educational too," Mom agreed.

"How is it educational?" I asked, terrified by the idea. "I'd much rather be outside riding a horse than inside reading about one."

My mother tousled my hair. "Because, Will, sometimes the only horse you can ride is the one in your head."

I had no idea what that meant.

"Don't make us join the library," Marty begged. "It's too dangerous."

"Dangerous? How could a library be dangerous?" Dad asked.

"It's not the library," Marty whispered. "It's the librarian."

"Mrs. Murphy?" said Mom. "She's a lovely old lady."

The problem with grown-ups is that they only see what's on the outside. But kids

know the real truth. People forget to be on their best behavior around kids, because nobody believes a word we say. Every kid in our town knew about Mrs. Murphy. She was one of those people that kids steer clear of. Like Miss White, the teacher with the evil eye, or old Ned Sawyer, the tramp with the drooling dog.

"She's not a lovely old lady," I said. "She's a total nut."

"Will! That's a terrible thing to say."

"But she is, Mom. She hates kids and she

used to be a spy in the army. Tracking kids from enemy countries."

"Now you're being ridiculous."

"She has a spud gun under her desk," added Marty. "A gas-powered one that takes an entire potato in the barrel. She shoots kids with it if they make a noise in the library. That's why we call her Spud Murphy."

My mother thought this was all very funny. "A spud gun! You'll say anything to avoid reading a book."

"It's true!" Marty shouted. "Do you know Ugly Frank, from number forty-seven?"

My mother tried to look stern. "You shouldn't call poor Frank ugly."

"Well, how do you think he got that way? Spud Murphy spudded him."

Mom waved her hands as if two annoying birds were flapping around her ears.

"I've heard enough. You two are going to

the library for the afternoon and that's it. We'll make some sandwiches."

We stood in the kitchen glumly. Sandwiches wouldn't be much use against Spud Murphy and her gas-powered spud gun.

STAY ON THE CARPET

Of course, the little brothers thought this was hilarious.

"Nice knowing you," said Donnie, shaking my hand.

"Yeth," said HP, the word whistling through the gap where his front teeth used to be. "Nithe knowing you."

Five years old and already a smart aleck.

"Can I have your Walkman?" asked Bert, who was already wearing it.

I swatted them with my Action Man. "Do you hear them, Mom? They're teasing us already."

"Oh, they don't mean it," said Mom. "Do you, my little men?"

"No, Mommy."

Mom gave them a gummi bear each. I thought my head would pop with the unfairness of it all.

"Now, Marty and Will, go upstairs and wash off the rest of my lipstick. We leave in ten minutes."

There was no escape. We pleaded and whined for ten minutes solid, but Mom was not giving an inch.

"The library will be good for you," she said, belting us tightly into the backseat of the car. "You might even learn something."

As we drove away, we looked back toward the house. Donnie was at the bedroom window, enacting a little play for our benefit. He had scrawled the name *Spud* across the front of his white T-shirt and was scolding a small figure standing on the window ledge. My heart jumped. It was Action Man. Donnie's scolding grew more and more furious, until eventually he picked up my unfortunate toy by the heels and began whacking him against the ledge.

"No," I squealed. "Stop the car. Donnie is killing Action Man."

Mom laughed. "Really, Will. Killing Action Man. You'll have to come up with something better than that."

Through the window I could see Bert and HP clapping wildly as Donnie took a bow.

Mom dropped us at the library on her way downtown.

"I'll pick you up on my way home, after I collect your dad from work."

We nodded, both too scared to talk.

Mom pointed her fingers at us like two imaginary guns.

"Try not to get spudded, okay?"

She was joking, but we couldn't laugh. We couldn't even manage a smile. Mom would be sorry when she came back, and our faces had been blasted by soggy potatoes.

"Okay, off you go, up the steps. I'll just stay here to make sure you go inside."

I growled quietly. Our plan had been to hide around the back for a few hours. Mom was smarter than we thought.

We climbed the concrete steps to the library doors. I decided to go first because Marty told me to. You're probably wondering what we were so scared about. I bet you're thinking that we were a pair of gutless chickens who would have been better off at home sewing our names onto handkerchiefs. But that's because you think libraries are happy colorful places, where the librarians actually like children. That may be what most of them are like, but this one was different. It was a place where serious men read serious books, and nobody was allowed to show even a glimmer of a smile. A smile could get you thrown out; a titter could get you spudded. And if you

laughed aloud, you were never seen again.

A little boy rushed out of the library, straight into Marty. The boy had tears coming out of his eyes, and someone had obviously been dragging him along by the collar.

He grabbed Marty's shirt. "Don't go in there," he cried. "For the love of God, don't do it. I was one day late with *Five Go to Smuggler's Top*. Just one day. And look what she did to me."

And just like that, the boy was gone, with only a puddle of tears to prove that he had ever been there.

"Wait," we cried after the fleeing figure. "Tell us what Spud did to you."

But it was no use. The boy had disappeared into the back of a dark car, which sped off to safety.

There was a porch outside the entrance to the library. The porch's walls were covered with posters about things like book groups and art competitions. All very educational. We looked at the pictures on the posters anyway. Anything to put off going into the library itself and facing Spud Murphy. We stayed there until Mom came up the steps and knocked on the window.

We had no choice but to go inside. It was just as I feared. There was nothing in there but books. Books just waiting to jump off the shelves and bore me silly. They seemed to watch me from their perches. I imagined them elbowing each other.

"Look," they said. "Two more kids having too much fun. We'll soon put a stop to that."

The library seemed to go on forever. Row after row of wooden bookshelves, bolted to the floor at the bottom and the ceiling at the top. Each row had a ladder with wheels on the upper end. Those ladders would have made great rides, but there was zero chance of children ever being allowed to actually have fun in here.

"What do you want?" said a voice from the other side of the library.

My heart speeded up at the very sound of that voice. It sounded like two pieces of rusted metal being rubbed together. I held my breath and looked across the huge room. An elderly woman was leaning on a huge wooden desk, her knuckles bigger

than acorns. Her gray hair was tied back so tightly that her eyebrows were halfway up her forehead. She looked surprised and angry at the same time. It was Spud Murphy, without a doubt.

"I said, what do you want?" she repeated, banging the desk with an ink stamp.

We walked across to her desk, clinging to each other like two frightened monkeys.

There was a whole box full of ink stamps on the desk, and two more hooked into her belt like six-shooters.

Spud Murphy glared down from a great height. She was big. Taller than my dad, and wider than Mom and my two aunties strapped together. Her arms were skinny like a robot's, and her eyes were like two black beetles behind her glasses.

"Mom says we have to join the library," I said. A full sentence. Not bad under the circumstances.

"That's all I need," grumbled Spud. "Two more urchins messing up my shelves." She took a pen and two cards from her drawer.

"Name?"

"M-M-Mrs. Murphy," I stammered.

Spud sighed. "Not my name, dummy. Your names."

"William and Martin Woodman!" I shouted, like an army cadet.

We had surrendered our names, and our address was next. I was a bit worried about that. Now Spud knew where we lived, and could track us down if we ever forgot to return a book.

The librarian filled in the cards, stamping them with the library crest.

"Pink cards," she said, handing them to

us. "Pink means junior. Pink means you stay in the junior section of the library."

Marty noticed that the toilets were in the grown-up section.

"What if we have to . . . go?"

Spud threw the stamp back in the box, slamming the lid.

"Think ahead," she said. "Go before you get here."

Spud led us down long aisles of wooden flooring to the junior section. She wore woolly slippers on her feet that polished the planks as she glided.

"That," she said, pointing a knobbly finger, "is the junior section."

The section was actually a single bookshelf with four rows of books. On the ground before it was a small patch of worn carpet.

"Do not set foot off that carpet until you leave," she warned. "Whatever boyish idea enters your head, ignore it. Stay on the carpet, or there will be trouble." She bent over almost double until her beetle eyes were level with my own. "Is that understood?"

I nodded. It was understood. No doubt about it.

THE TEST

On that first day on the carpet, Marty decided that we should test Spud. When Spud said there would be trouble if we stepped off the carpet, what exactly did she mean? Did trouble mean a strict talking-to? Or did trouble mean being suspended by your fingernails over a pit of alligators?

"I need to know how much I can get away with," said Marty, tying his sweater around his neck like a bib.

"I don't need to know," I said, remembering the boy who had run past us in hysterics. "I'll just sit here and pretend to read."

"You are such a chicken," said Marty. "No wonder Action Man is your only friend. I, on the other hand, am an actual hero type. I am prepared to take risks."

"Why did you tie your sweater to your chest?"

"Wait and see, chicken boy," said Marty.

My big brother walked around the edge of the carpet, checking to see if Spud would spot him.

"She can't even see us," he said. "We can do whatever we want."

I was starting to get worried. Whenever a boy did something wrong, grown-ups tended to blame the entire family. "What are you going to do?" I asked.

Marty smiled. "The best way to mess with a librarian is to put things back in the wrong place." He rubbed his hands gleefully. "They hate that. It drives them nuts." Marty was an expert on messing with librarians. There had been several notes home from the school library. "So I'm just going to switch a few books for Mrs. Spud Murphy. By the time she finds out, we'll be home watching cartoons."

Marty lay on his stomach and wiggled out

onto the wooden floor. He glided across the polished planks on a double layer of wool. I had to admit it. Marty was a master.

Like a crocodile swimming down the Nile, Marty slid to the nearest bookshelf with barely a sound. He climbed onto the bottom shelf, and perched there motionless. There was only one other person at this end of the library—a short man with gray hair and bushy eyebrows. Marty waited until he moved away before he began causing mischief.

One book at a time, he switched almost every single book in the section. He put mysteries with romance, adventure with bird-watching, and gardening with model airplanes. Spud would be furious. To make matters worse, Marty started to swap the reference sheets at the end of each shelf. These pages told the reader what kind of book was on that particular shelf. Marty

reached up slowly and tore the sheet from the clip that held it.

Suddenly, a shadow fell across my brother. It was a big sharp shadow, and it belonged to a big sharp person. I turned to look. It was Spud. She had appeared without a sound, like a ninja librarian.

Spud stood, slippered feet apart, with her hands hovering over the book stamps on her belt. Marty hadn't seen her, and was still holding the reference page. It was too late to warn him. There was nothing I could do.

Spud's left hand moved with lightning speed, grabbing a book stamp and throwing it in one smooth precise motion. It tumbled through the air so fast that it hissed. Marty turned just in time to see the block of wood and rubber heading in his direction.

It was too late to move out of the way. All Marty could do was close his eyes and squeal like a kitten.

The rubber stamp snagged the reference page in Marty's hand, plucking it from his fingers and stamping it against the shelf. The force of the throw was so strong that the page stayed there for several seconds after the stamp had fallen to the ground. Two words were stamped on the page in purple ink: DAMAGED GOODS.

"I knew it," said Spud slowly. "I can always tell a troublemaker. I took one look at you, Master Martin Woodman, and I knew you'd be off that carpet before I was back at my desk."

"You set me up," said Marty, surprised.

"That's right. I was waiting behind the shelf. The sweater trick was good, but I've tracked a lot sneakier than you in my day."

Marty stood slowly, no sudden moves.

"I'm sorry, Spu—Mrs. Murphy. I'll never leave the carpet again."

Spud slid across the floor on her slippers. "Too late for that. Since you're already off the carpet, you can fix the damage you've done."

"But there are hundreds of books. I can't remember them all."

Spud ran a finger along the shelf. "Each book has a number. This section starts at number five hundred and sixty." She plucked a book from the shelf. "Here it is. I've started you off. You get these in order by the time your mother comes to pick you up, and maybe I won't have to tell her how you set off the fire alarms."

Marty's mouth flapped. "But . . . I didn't."

Spud put her hands on her hips. "I know you didn't, and I'm sure your mother will believe that. Unless, of course, you've been in trouble before."

Marty thought about it for a moment, then began rearranging books as fast as he could. He knew when he'd met his match.

Two hours and fourteen paper cuts later, Marty was finished. He sat on the carpet sucking his fingers.

"That wasn't so bad," he said on the way to the exit. "I've had teachers meaner than her."

Marty was actually getting cocky again.

"Marty! Don't you remember the rubber stamp? She nearly took your head off."

"Yes. That was cool. She must practice for hours. Do you think she'll really say that I set off the fire alarms?"

"I don't care," I said. "I just want to get out of here."

Marty had started to wander over toward Spud. I couldn't believe it. Mom was outside, waiting in the car. I could see her through the swinging doors. We were almost safe, and Marty was going over to the librarian's desk.

"Excuse me, Mrs. Murphy."

Spud's head swiveled slowly, like a tank gun. Her eyes landed on Marty.

"Martin Woodman. Back for more. I

would have thought you'd keep well away from me."

"Just one question, Mrs. Murphy. You wouldn't really say I set off the alarms, would you?"

Spud smiled back at Marty. Her teeth looked like a row of icicles.

"Oh, wouldn't I?"

"I don't think so. Throwing a stamp is one thing. That was cool, by the way."

"You liked that, did you, Martin?"

"Sure did."

Spud opened the box on her desk. "I have a collection of stamps here. One came in last week you might like. It's in the shape of a pirate flag. A lot of the boys like me to stamp it onto their forearms, like a temporary tattoo." She began to close the box. "But maybe you're too young."

Marty was already rolling up his sleeve. "No. I'd love that. On my arm. Wait until

the guys at the swimming pool see this."

Spud selected a stamp, inking it on a blue pad.

"Are you sure, Martin? This won't wash off for a couple of weeks."

"I'm sure. Stamp away."

"Well, if you're sure."

Spud's smile widened. "Okay then. Keep still." The librarian rolled the rubber stamp across Marty's forearm. Across and back, three times. When she removed the stamp, we leaned in to examine the pirate flag. Only it wasn't a pirate flag. It was a short sentence of three words. The words were: I LOVE BARBIE.

"Oops," said Spud. "Wrong stamp. Sorry about that."

Marty couldn't speak. If anyone saw those words on his forearm, he'd be teased for all eternity.

"You boys had better hurry up," said

Spud, placing the stamp back in the box. "One more thing. Any more of your little games and I get nasty. There are worse things in this desk than rubber stamps."

We walked to the door. Marty held his arm in front of him as though it belonged to someone else.

Spud called to him as he opened the door. "Oh, Martin," she said, "enjoy swimming."

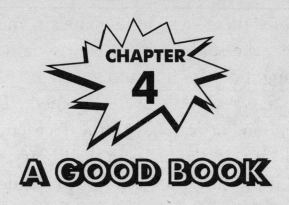

CHAPTER 4

A GOOD BOOK

For the next few visits, I sat on the carpet pretending to read. I sat there until I felt sure the pattern from that faded old carpet had transferred itself onto my bottom. Marty spent most of the time licking his forearm, but it was no use. The stamp didn't fade, and now he had a blue tongue, too. Sometimes Mom arrived early to take us home and would catch me pretending to read.

"Now, there's a sight to make any mother smile," she said. "I knew you would love reading if only you would give it a try."

That was it. We were doomed. Three afternoons a week, Mom decided, we would spend two hours in the library.

So three times a week we pretended to read quietly. Sometimes we forgot to be quiet, and then Spud would pay the children's section a visit. I remember the first time it happened. We were arguing over who owned the air in our bedroom. I said that Marty owned the air on his side of the room, but he said that he owned the air at ground level. This meant that I would have to climb onto the top bunk just to breathe.

Suddenly, a familiar shadow fell across the carpet, making me shiver. Spud stood there, feet apart, belt weighed down with rubber stamps. Without saying a thing, she pulled out a large flash card from her pocket. On the flash card was written the word *Shhh*. We got the message.

We couldn't fight, we couldn't shout, we couldn't make loud bodily noises. All the things young boys live for. Oh, the boredom! My head felt like it would fall off and spin across the wooden floor. I tried everything to entertain myself. Watching movies in my head, following the pattern in my carpet prison, eating strips of paper from the books. But most of all, I just dreamed of freedom.

Then one day, something strange happened. I was pretending to read a book called *Finn McCool the Giant of Ireland*, when something caught my eye. It was the first sentence of the story.

Finn McCool, it said, *was the biggest giant in Ireland*.

There was something about that sentence. It was . . . interesting. I decided to read a bit more. I wouldn't read the whole book, no way. But maybe just another couple of sentences.

Finn had a problem, said the book. *Angus MacTavish, the biggest giant in Scotland, wanted to fight him.*

Well, I couldn't stop now. Two giants fighting! Maybe I'd just see how that turned out. And so I read to the end of the page, and then I kept right on reading. Before I knew it, I was lost in the tale of Finn McCool and

Angus MacTavish. There was adventure and magic and battles and clever plans. Mountains exploded and wizards slew goblins. Magic goats talked and princesses turned into swans. It was another world.

"Ready to go?" said a voice.

I looked up. It was Mom.

"What are you doing here?" I asked.

There were shopping bags in Mom's hands. "What do you think I'm doing here? It's time to go."

I hugged the book to my chest. "But we just got here. It's only . . ."

I stopped talking, because I had spotted

the wall clock. It was five o'clock. I had been reading a book for almost two hours. I looked across at Marty. He was still reading! A book with a picture of a dragon on the cover. What was going on here?

"Come on now, your dad will be waiting."

To my complete amazement, I realized that I didn't want to leave my book behind. And neither did Marty.

"But, Mom . . ."

"Yes, Marty?"

"I haven't finished my book."

"Neither have I."

Mom put down the shopping bags, and gave us both a big hug. Right out in public. It's a good thing our friends didn't hang out in libraries.

"Do you think Spu—eh . . . Mrs. Murphy would let us bring them home?"

Mom picked up the bags. "Of course. You have your cards, don't you?"

CHAPTER 5

OFF THE CARPET

For weeks, everything was wonderful. We had the time of our lives. Every new book opened the door to a new world. We floated down the great Mississippi River with Huckleberry Finn. Robin Hood taught us how to shoot a bow and arrow. We caught burglars with the Famous Five, and Stig of the Dump gave us fort-building tips.

Spud Murphy generally left us alone, so long as we returned our books on time and didn't make any noise on the carpet. A few times she had to show us the *Shhh* flash card, but we never got up to any real mischief. Until . . .

One Monday, we ran out of books to read. We had read everything twice, even the Nancy Drew mysteries. We sat on the carpet dreading the boredom that would soon set in. It wasn't fair.

Marty was so bored he was licking his forearm again, even though the Barbie stamp was long gone.

He stopped licking to complain. "What are we going to do?" he moaned. "I can't sit here for six hours a week with no books."

"Me neither."

"It's such a tragedy. The adventure section is right over there."

"The *adult* adventure section. We only have pink cards, remember?"

"I know, but if one of us just had the guts

to go over there. . . One book is all we need to get us through the afternoon."

I covered my head with a book. "No way. Don't even ask. I'm not listening."

Marty crawled over to me. "Oh, come on. I can't go. Spud has her eye on me."

"But what about the spud gun?"

Marty pinched my cheek. "You're the cute one. If Spud catches you, she'll probably give you a lollipop."

"No, Marty," I whispered in case Spud heard.

"I'll let you breathe my air in the bedroom."

"No."

"I'll let you hang around with me and the boys."

"I don't want to hang around with you."

"I'll tell you where Action Man is buried."

I gasped. "Action Man is buried?" I had been so distracted with my books that I hadn't even noticed he was missing!

Marty knew he had me. "Yes. Somewhere in the garden. The big garden. I'd say the worms are starting to nibble on him around now."

What choice did I have? Action Man

needed me, and I did really want something to read.

"Okay, Marty," I hissed. "I'll go. But only today. If you want a book on Wednesday, you'll have to go yourself."

Marty patted me on the shoulder. "That's fair," he said. "'Now, off you go. I want something really exciting."

I put one foot off the carpet, onto the wooden floor. It creaked like a bat squealing. Seconds later, Spud skated around the corner, her slippers gliding over the polished planks.

Shhh, said her card.

"Sorry," I whispered.

Spud's beetle eyes squinted at us suspiciously, but she continued on to the romance section.

"I knew you couldn't do it, chicken boy," said Marty. "Not even when Action Man is counting on you."

I stuck my tongue out at Marty. I wasn't beaten yet, not with Action Man buried in the garden. I would show Marty that I was no chicken boy. I stripped off my shoes and socks and tried again. With utmost care I lowered my big toe onto the boards, like a mouse testing a trap. No creak. Just beautiful silence. This could work. There were no adults at this end of the library, so I only had Spud to worry about. I took one little step. Then one more.

Every boy knows that if you want to cross a floor silently, then stick close to the wall. I stuck so close that I could almost feel my shadow tickling my back. Inch by inch, I made my way toward the adventure section. Every patch of skin on my body was sweating. It felt as though my teeth were sweating. What would Spud Murphy do if she caught me? Would I get the stamp, or the spud gun? Spud gun, I guessed. After all, Marty had already received the family warning.

A ladder blocked my way. A library ladder with wheels on the top. I needed this ladder to reach the adventure books. Gently I wheeled it along the shelves toward the adventure section. It didn't squeak once. Spud kept her ladders well oiled.

I could see the books now, just out of reach. I climbed the ladder slowly, waiting for the creak that would bring Spud running. One step, then two, then three. High enough to reach for a book. I made myself as tall as I could, stretching from the tip of my big toe to the point of my index finger. I took a book from the shelf and stuffed it down the back of my trousers. Success. All that remained was the return journey to the carpet.

The trip back was just as scary. I was sweating so much that I began to feel thirsty. The distance between me and the carpet seemed ten times longer than it had on the way over, and every tiny sound I made echoed around the high walls. But I couldn't stop now. If I did, Spud would surely catch me on her next round. Then I would be spudded for sure. So I took step after sweaty step until the ladder was back in its place, and I was safe on the carpet.

Marty pulled the book out of my trousers. "Well done, Will. I didn't think you had it in you."

"Now, tell me," I demanded, "where is Action Man buried?"

Marty grinned. "In the toy box, sucker, where he always is."

My big brother had tricked me again, but I was too relieved to be angry.

We took a look at the book's cover. *Spies in Siberia*, it said across the top in gold letters. Underneath there was a picture of a man skiing down a snowy mountain. Spud could tell from a hundred yards that this was no kid's book. So Marty borrowed a cover from one of the children's books and folded it over *Spies in Siberia*.

I put my shoes and socks back on, and

then we read happily for the rest of the afternoon. Those spies had a fine time with their fast cars and parachutes and kissing every girl they met. I could have done without the kissing, but the rest was great. It was the first time I had ever been this close to Marty for any length of time without an argument breaking out.

At four-thirty, Marty hid *Spies in Siberia*

behind a row of Enid Blytons, and we settled back to wait for Mom. I have to admit
that I was feeling very pleased with
myself. I had outwitted the famous Spud
Murphy. Her tracking skills had been no
match for my brain. I was the King of the
Library.

Or was I?

Suddenly Spud glided round the corner

on her woolly slippers. She skidded to a stop before us, sniffing the air like one of those mean pit bull dogs. Her eyebrows seemed even higher than usual.

"Something's not right," she said in her rusted metal voice.

We smiled innocently. Like most boys, we did a great innocent smile.

Spud glared at us. "Innocent smiles don't

work on me, little men. Unless you really are innocent. Which I doubt."

I could feel my smile shrinking, like a banana being gobbled up from both ends. Stay calm, I told myself. Thirty minutes, and Mom will be here to save us.

Spud skated around the library floor in large circles, looking for something out of place. Her eyes flitted across the polished wood, like an eagle's searching for a mouse. Finally, she came to the spot where I had started my journey. She skated past it.

Whew.

Then, stopped and turned back.

Oh no.

Something had caught Spud's eye. Something in the exact spot where I had stood. She bent low to the ground, and followed my path to the ladder.

"Coincidence," whispered Marty, from the corner of his mouth. "Don't worry."

Spud placed one hand on the ladder, pushing it along the shelves. She stopped at the adventure section.

This couldn't be happening.

The librarian climbed to the third step, and reached out one knobbly finger. The finger pointed to a space on the shelf.

"Aha," she said.

I couldn't believe it. She must have some magical powers. I was in deep trouble. The deepest.

Spud climbed down and skated over to the carpet. She stopped before us and said three words.

"*Spies in Siberia*?"

I tried my innocent smile again. "Pardon?"

"*Spies in Siberia*. One of you took it from the adventure section. Hand it over."

By now I was too scared to speak actual words. I did manage to shake my head. *No*, the shake said, *it wasn't me*.

Marty did a bit better. "I would never ignore library rules and leave the children's section," he said, straight-faced. "That would be wrong and my parents would be so disappointed."

Spud squinted at us through beetle eyes. "So, that's the way it is," she said. "Okay, then, I want both of you to lie down."

We obeyed, and with deft movements, she whipped off our shoes and socks. She studied our bare feet, and eventually settled on me.

"Stand up," she ordered.

I did as I was told. Wouldn't you if Spud Murphy was looming over you?

Spud tucked her hands under my arms, lifting me fifteen inches straight up in the air.

"I think it was you, William," she said. "Because you left a trail."

What trail? I couldn't have left a trail.

Spud glided over to the wall where I had begun my journey, and set me down right on my own sweaty footprints. I had left a trail all right. A trail of drying footprints.

"Now," she said sternly, "hand over *Spies in Siberia*."

I was caught. Fair and square. The evidence was against me. What could I do but return the book and beg for mercy? I trudged back to the children's section and took my borrowed book from the shelves.

Marty shook his head in disgust. "Shame on you," he said. "How could you break library rules?"

I ignored him, too busy wondering what terrible punishment Spud would inflict on me.

"Here," I said, handing her *Spies in Siberia*.

Spud shook her head in wonder.

"Why did you do it? Aren't you terrified of me? All the other children are."

At that moment, I made the best decision of the afternoon. I told the truth, or at least some of it.

"I wanted a book," I said in a shaky voice. "I had read all the others, most of them twice. I had to get a book."

"Even though you knew I might catch you?"

My bottom lip was trembling like Jell-O. "It was worth the risk."

"Right!" said Spud. "Stand in front of my desk. I have something for you. And it's not a rubber stamp."

Oh no! The gas-powered spud gun. I was
going to get spudded. Time to beg.

"But . . ."

Spud raised her hand. "No buts. You're
going to get what you deserve. Go on, in
front of my desk."

I walked to the desk, more frightened than I had ever been in my life. This was it, the end of my time as a cute kid. From today on I would be known as Weird Will, the Spud-faced Kid. It was too much. I closed my eyes so I wouldn't see it coming.

My ears kept right on working, supplying noises for my imagination to add pictures to. Behind me, Marty was still making *tsk tsk* sounds of disgust, as though I had let him down. In front of me I heard Spud rooting around in her desk drawer. She was probably loading the spud gun, picking a really hard potato.

"Open your eyes!" she ordered.

"No," I moaned. "I can't."

"Come on, William Woodman. Look at what I've got for you!"

I took a deep breath and opened my eyes. Instead of the barrel of a spud gun, there was a blue card in front of my eyes. Behind the card was Spud's face. She was smiling and her teeth didn't remind me of icicles anymore. They looked friendly.

"A blue library card," she said. "Blue means adult. Blue means you can go anywhere you want in the library. All I ask is that you show me any adult books you pick, so I can check if they're suitable for you."

I was amazed. Could Spud be rewarding me for breaking the rules?

"W-w-why?" I stammered.

Spud smiled again. It quite suited her face.

"Because you left the carpet for a book. Not to cause mischief. Books are what this library is for. Sometimes even I forget that."

Wow. I had done something good, by accident. Wait till Mom heard about this.

Spud winked at me. "Maybe it's time I expanded the children's section, and got rid of that carpet."

I thought about it. "Maybe you could leave the carpet where it is. But just as somewhere to sit."

Spud put out her hand. "It's a deal."

I shook her bony hand. Winking and hand-shaking? Maybe aliens had abducted the librarian and left this Spud-shaped robot in her place.

"Mrs. Murphy, seeing as we're so friendly now, would it be okay if I called you Spud?"

The librarian put her free hand under the desk. She twisted something, and whatever she had under there began to hiss gently.

"Just try it once, Woodman, and see what happens."

I backed away slowly.

"Maybe I'll just wait for Mom on the carpet."

"Good idea."

Now, I know what you're thinking. Surely after Marty's terrible behavior I would stay well out of his reach. Well, you're nearly right. I did stay out of his reach, about fifteen inches out of his reach. I stood a yard off the carpet and waved the blue adult card at him.

"Get me a book," he begged.

"After that Action Man trick you pulled? Forget it."

"Come on. You can breathe the bedroom air."

"Well, okay," I said, and brought him *Roses in Autumn* from the romance section.

"Not this one," he cried, reading the back cover. "I don't want a book about someone called Penelope."

I was already halfway up the adventure section. I cupped one hand around my ear as though I couldn't hear him, and he didn't dare shout. When I glanced Marty's way, a few minutes later, he was twenty pages into the romance novel.

At ten past four, a horn beeped three times outside. One long beep, two short beeps. Our signal. Mom was waiting. We quickly chose books to take home. Marty was borrowing *Roses in Autumn*.

"There's a lot of sword fighting," he said as Spud stamped the book.

Spud stamped my book, too, and slipped my blue library card into a little envelope.

"You know, Will, now that we're so friendly, maybe you could call me Angela."

I tucked my book under one arm.

"See you Wednesday, Angela," I said.

Spud smiled. "See you Wednesday, Will."

And she did.

Don't miss

EOIN COLFER'S
Legend of . . .
CAPTAIN CROW'S TEETH

After surviving a summer with ninja librarian Spud Murphy, not much can scare Will and Marty Woodman. Until, that is, they travel with their family to a small seaside town famous for its resident ghost. Legend has it that when the rocks beneath the sea glow at night, pirate Captain Augustine Crow haunts the shore searching for a new cabin boy.

Of course, nine-year-old Will knows this can't be true. But one night, he is out late, and the sea is lit with an eerie glow . . . and, is that a ghostly voice calling his name?

Eoin Colfer is a former elementary school teacher who made a splash in the book world with the internationally best-selling Artemis Fowl series. His other popular books include *The Supernaturalist* and *The Wish List*.

To learn more about Eoin Colfer, visit his Web site at www.eoincolfer.com

Glenn McCoy is an award-winning cartoonist and animator. He has twice been named the Magazine Cartoonist of the Year by the National Cartoonists Society. He is also the creator of the book *Penny Lee and Her TV*. Glenn lives in Illinois with his family.